:MY BOOK:

For Christy,
who always has
ideas to inspire me.
S.M.

HUGO & MILES IN I've Painted everything!

SCOTT MAGOON

Houghton Mifflin Company

Boston 2007

In the small city of Cornville there lived a very creative artist named Hugo.

One afternoon, he had just finished a painting.
"That's it!" he said proudly as he finished it.
"I've painted everything!"

But
something
was
wrong.

Hugo looked over his hundreds of paintings. "I painted this, and that, and those . . . and him, and her, here, there, and everywhere."

He went to meet his best friend, Miles, for help.

They ordered the usual. Peanut butter burgers.

"I have nothing to do," sighed Hugo, "because I've painted everything!"

"Hugo, you are in an elephunk," said Miles. "Let's go on a trip. I have very important business in Paris this week as I test one

of my latest inventions. Come with me ... you might be inspired to paint something new."

"I don't know, Miles. It's so far away. I'm not sure ..."

"Nonsense! Whenever I go on a trip," said Miles, "I think of new things as I see sights I've never seen. You will too. Trust me."

So they flew to Paris.

They spent days exploring the whole city.

They went to a huge art museum called the Louvre.

"I've never painted that big," exclaimed Hugo.

"What if I did?"

"Then your painting would be Hugo-mongous."

"Hmmm . . ." said Hugo.

They had a picnic.

"What if I just painted a solid color?" asked Hugo.

"Then you would be Hue-Go."

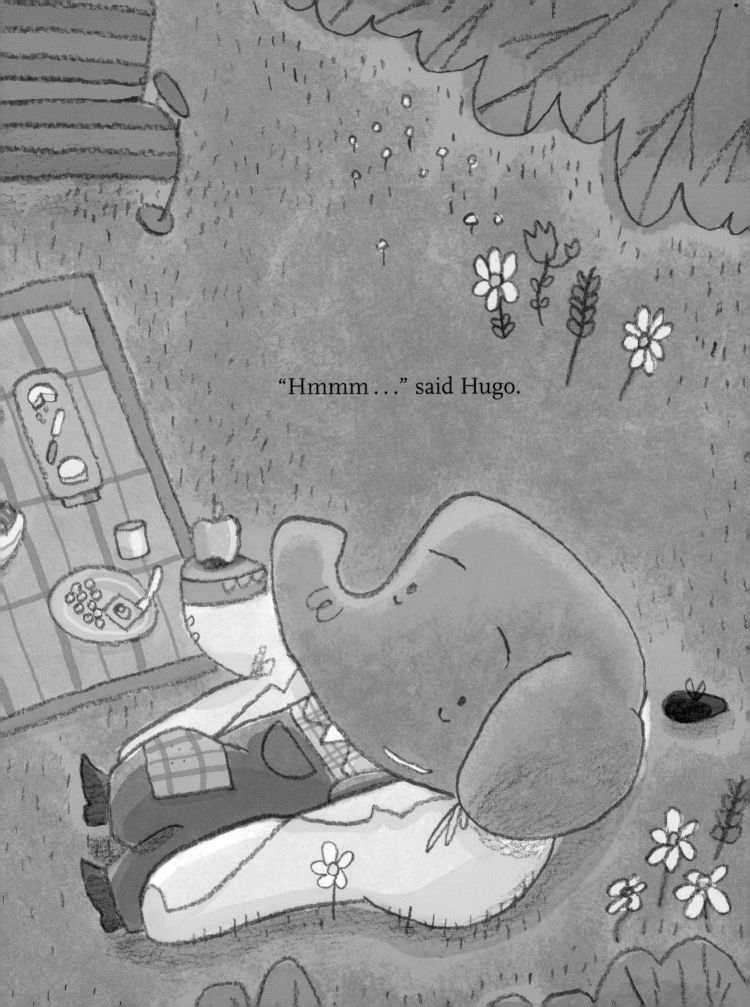

"Hmmm..." said Hugo.

They went to the Musée d'Orsay.

"What if I painted an impression of how I felt?"

"Then you'd be Van Hugo."

"Hmmm..." said Hugo.

And on the evening before their last day
in Paris, they sat to talk.

"What if I painted with light?"

"Hu-glow."

"Oh, Miles, this has been a fun trip,
but I'm afraid I still don't know what to paint."

"Only one thing left to do," said Miles.
"Tomorrow, come up the Eiffel Tower with me."

The next morning, they climbed to the top of the tower. The city looked entirely different than it had over the past few days.

Suddenly, Hugo looked up and exclaimed,

"Miles, we've got to go home!" shouted Hugo.

"But Hugo—"

"No, come on, back to Cornville."

"What is it? What is your idea?"
asked Miles.

"It's been right in front of my trunk all along,"
Hugo replied. "I painted this, and that, and
those . . . and him, and her, and it, here, there,
and everywhere . . ."

"...but not from here."

Miles gasped. "Wow, Cornville looks so different!"

"Yes," exclaimed Hugo. "See, I thought I painted everything, but I haven't. My idea is that I can paint everything all over again, only differently."

"From here above,

or here below...

I can use one color…

paint an impression…

or use light instead of paint."

"I can change the size of my canvas to be Hugo-mongous, or even . . .

. . . very small. Miles, if I just change the way I look at things,
I'll never run out of ideas," said Hugo.

And he never did.

www.houghtonmifflinbooks.com

The text of this book is set in 18-point Scala.
The illustrations are created with pencil and digitally colored.

Library of Congress Cataloging-in-Publication Data
Magoon, Scott.
Hugo & Miles in I've painted everything! / written and illustrated by Scott Magoon.
p. cm.
Summary: When elephant artist Hugo develops artist's block, his friend Miles convinces
him to go along on a trip to Paris, where Hugo learns to see things in new ways.
ISBN-13: 978-0-618-64638-8 (hardcover)
ISBN-10: 0-618-64638-8 (hardcover)
[1. Artists—Fiction. 2. Art museums—Fiction. 3. Museums—Fiction. 4. Elephants—
Fiction. 5. Paris (France)—Fiction. 6. France—Fiction.] I. Title. II. Title: Hugo and Miles.
III. Title: I've painted everything. IV. Title: I have painted everything.
PZ7.M31266513Hug 2007   [E]—dc22   2006009818

Printed in Singapore
TWP   10   9   8   7   6   5   4   3   2   1

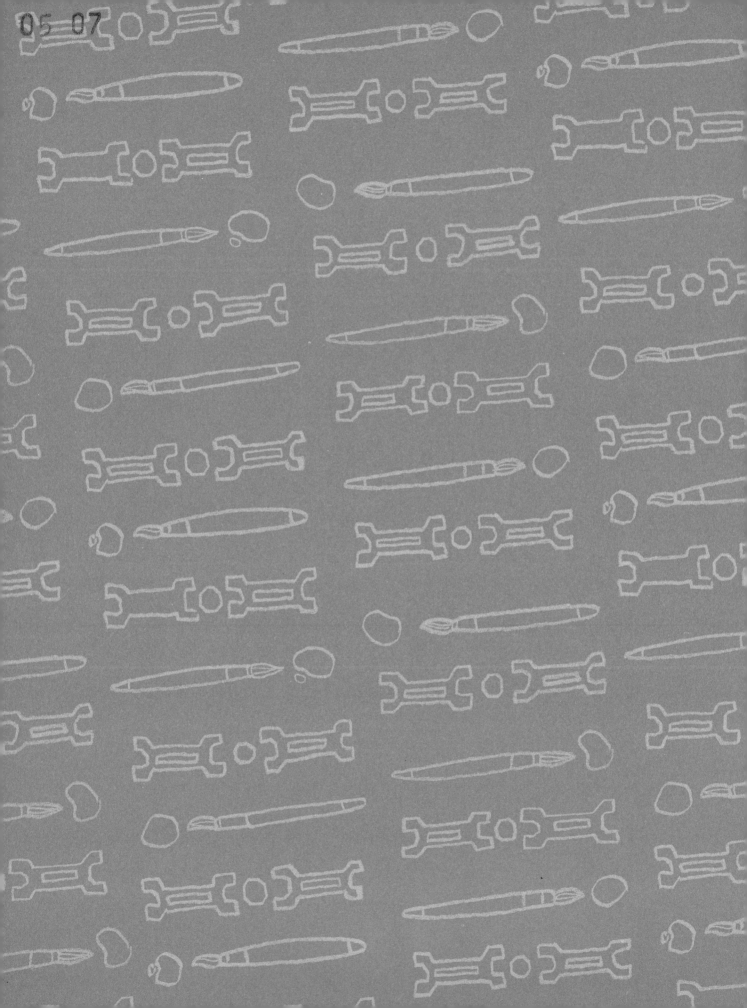